STORY BY KATHRYN LASKY · PAINTINGS BY ROCCO BAVIERA

FIRST PAINTER

DK
Ink

DORLING KINDERSLEY PUBLISHING, INC.

he Moon of the Singing Grass has come and gone three times, and still there is no rain. Babies have been born and grown into little walkers and never seen rain.

My name is Mishoo. I have lived for ten Moons of the Singing Grass, and now I am beginning to forget the rain—its sound, its shape, and how the water clouds gather like herds of woolly mammoths in the east.

My people are hungry. They are starving. First the grass died, then the animals. Now us.

My mother was a Dream Catcher
who spoke with the spirits. She came
from the people of Cloud River. The
Cloud River clans are known for their
Dream Catchers. My mother died in
the Moon of the Red Dust, trying to
catch a dream of rain and meat for
her people. So now I, Mishoo, as
eldest daughter, am the Dream
Catcher.

My younger sister, Erloo, is so thin her wrists are like twigs. Every time I have painted the spirit stripes on my arms, she has looked at me, hoping I will catch a dream, a dream of rain and meat and tender shoots to chew and bushes bursting with berries. But the stripes have not brought any of this.

Before my mother died she gave me her spirit bundle. In it are small packets of dried, colored muds and clay dug from the river—these are the colors of the earth. The sky colors we pick from the berry bushes that grow along the river during the Moon of the Fat Berries. Except now the berries have withered and the river has run dry, and there is little water to make the Dream Catcher's marks on my body as my mother had done and her mother before her.

So the time of hunger goes on. Nothing will bring the rain. And my sister grows thinner and thinner on the hopes of dreams I cannot catch.

I go to sleep weary and frightened, but even my sleep gives me no rest. For every night the spirit of my mother and her mother and her mother's mother visit. . . .

Mishoo, Mishoo, they call. *You must go to the cave of the she-tiger.*

I cannot believe that my mother's and grandmothers' spirits would tell me to do such a dangerous thing. So I try to forget.

But they come back again and again.

Look at your sister, they say. *She will never live through the winter.*

You are the Dream Catcher now, Mishoo. You must go. You must go to the cave of the she-tiger.

The words swirl like colors in my mind's eye. There is no choice. I must go.

The cave is well hidden in the mountain. On the path I see the footprints of tigers and their claw marks on the trees. I must talk my feet forward.

The opening is a narrow crack in the rock, and I squeeze through it. The she-tiger must press herself thin as a beaver to slide in.

Then I slither on my belly beneath a stone ledge. The light vanishes, and I am swallowed by the darkness. I crawl through a tunnel for the lengths of more hunting men than my hands have fingers. The smell of wet clay fills my nose. Finally the tunnel opens into a big cave thick with the musk of the she-tiger's spirit.

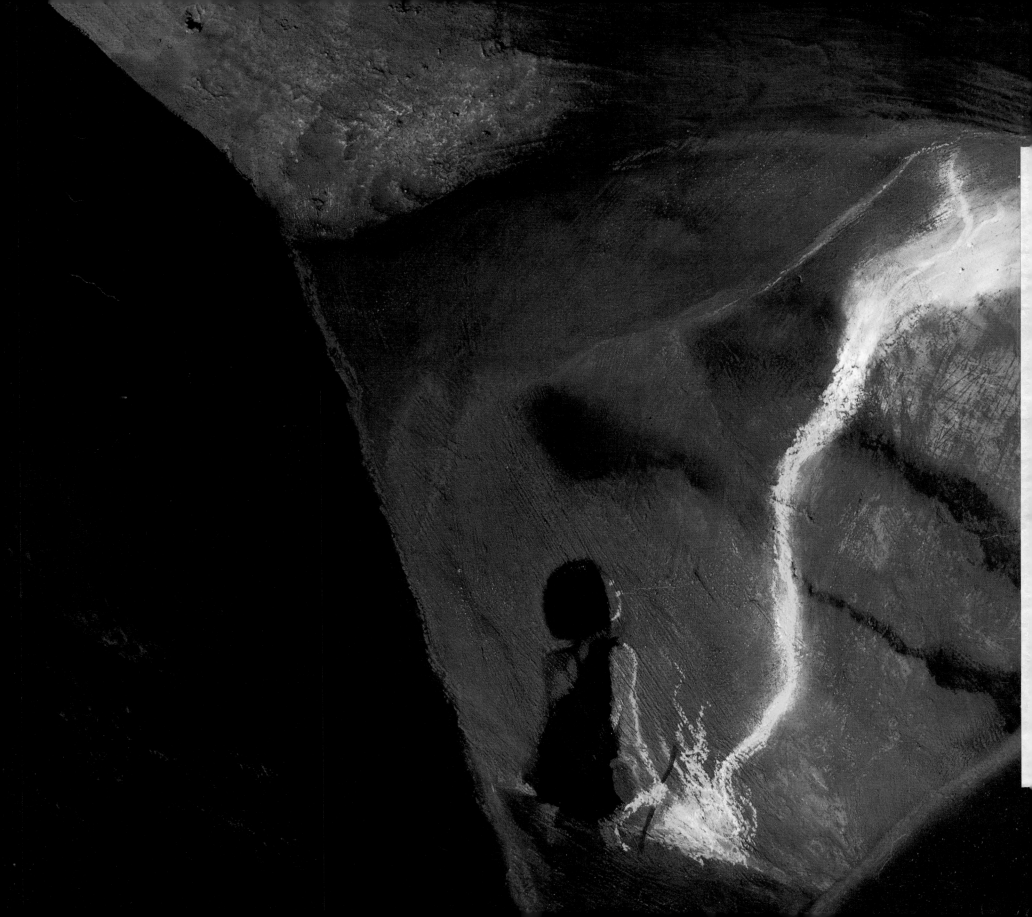

I take out my fire sticks and roll a fire. My heart quickens. I have never seen such rock! There are rocks that look like dripping animal fat and rocks that glitter with small crystals like frozen water. There are spears of rock like giant fangs from the saber-toothed tiger.

I open my spirit bundle and wait. . . . What am I to do? Should I make the stripes thinner this time? Should I paint the ring around my navel? The colors swirl with the scent of the tiger. My fingers shake. I won't be able to make the marks. I want to leave, but I think of Erloo's thin twig arms.

The shadows dance on the wall. The rock breathes. I begin to hear the lost herds of animals, like distant thunder; their spirits dim in the rock.

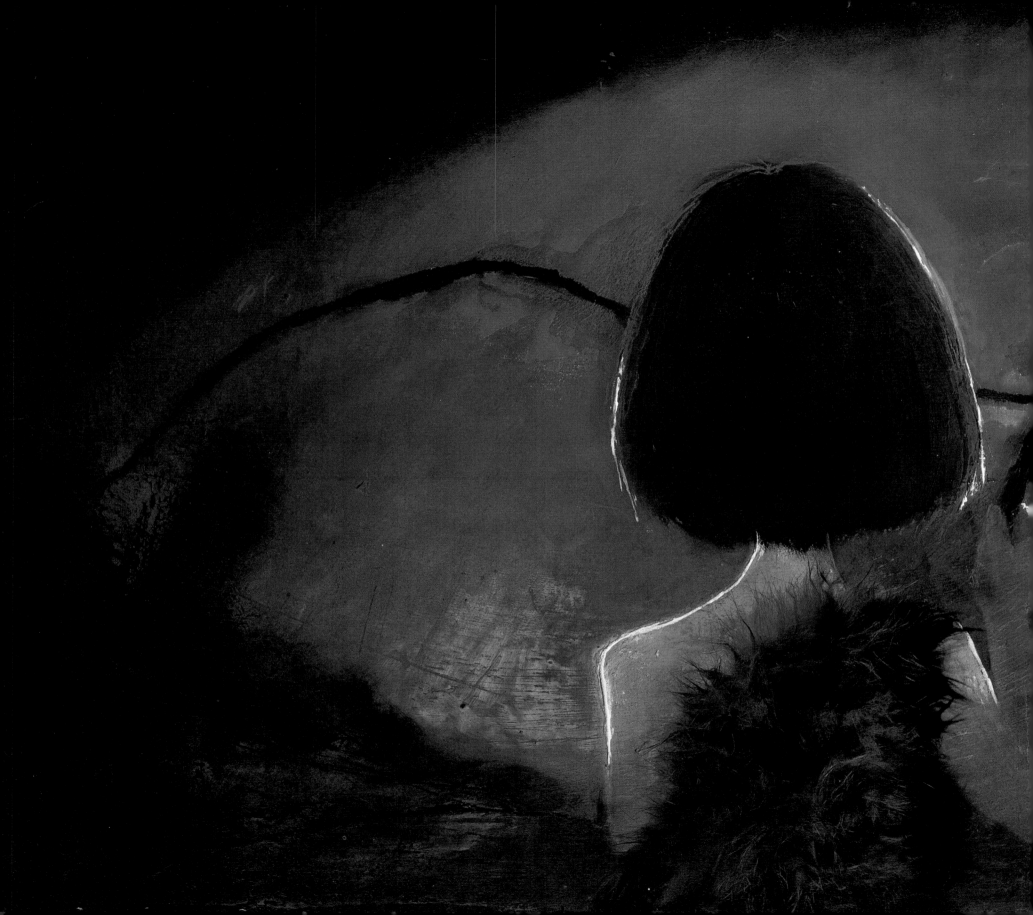

Then I catch the flickerings of fire on the walls. Suddenly the rock comes alive with sliding shadows. Something stirs in my mind's eye.

I pick up a charred stick from the fire. I trace the outline of the horse's head buried in the stone and follow the pale gray vein to draw the horse's back. I can see the curve of the rump and where the running leg joins it.

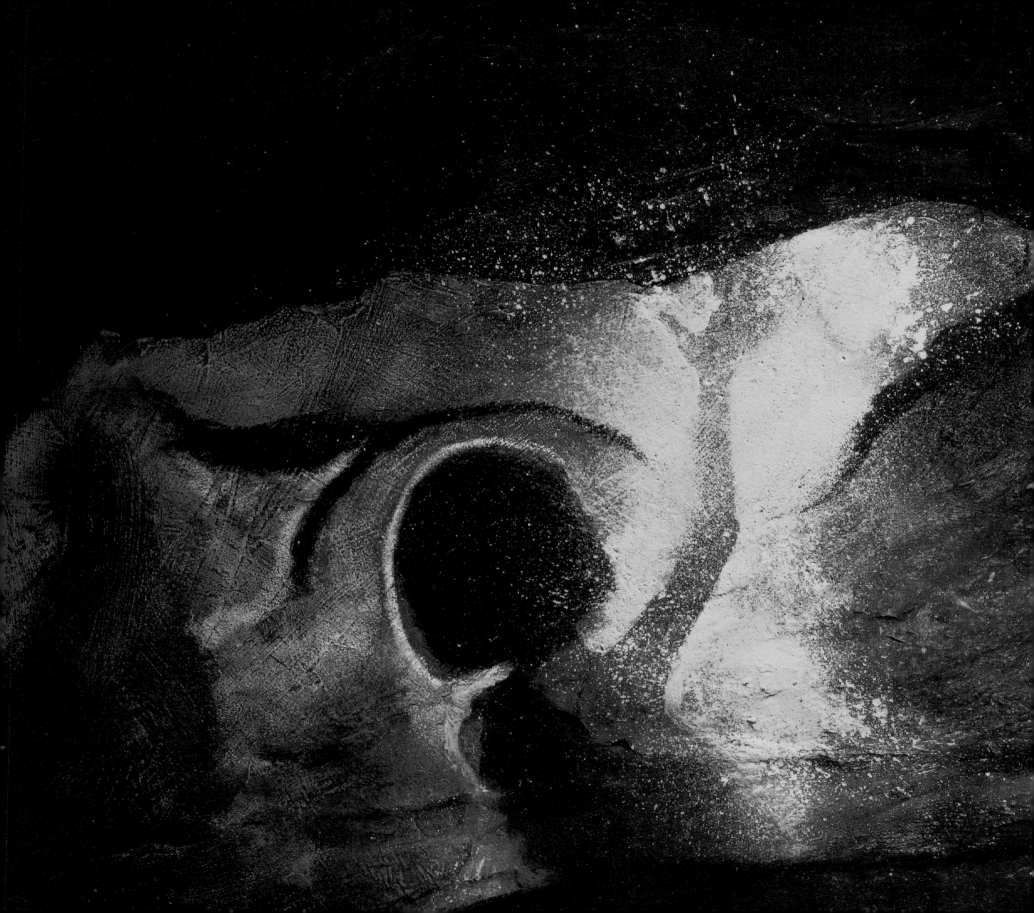

I stand back and look. This is not just a galloping horse! It sweats. Its eyes slide with wildness. Its muscles strain with speed. I take the ocher powder from my spirit bundle and then feel a tickle in my nose. I lift my hand to stop a sneeze—too late! A palmful of yellow powder sprays against the wall. Like mist, the tiny beads of color settle on the horse's rump. I like that. I put some ocher in my mouth, then blow it out like another sneeze.

When I blow I feel my spirit join that of the running horse. I feel the heartbeat of the horse. I feel the strength of its pounding legs, its speed. I feel bigger, stronger.

Am I catching spirits or being caught myself?

I sleep well that night. By early morning I have rolled my fire in the cave and begun to paint a whole herd of horses. They do not look as if they are running as fast as the ones that streak the plains. I think hard about this, I close my eyes tight and picture the herds pounding the earth. I see many legs, but never one clearly. That is the way running legs are! In the stillness of the cave, I keep this image of running.

So now I make many legs, more than the horses really need. I paint them soft and misty. These are running legs. I feel the speed. I hear the hooves.

All day I work. I paint. I smudge. I blow the color and trace with my stick until I am too tired to do more.

But I begin to see another animal in the rock. In the spirit bundle I find the angry red from the upper banks of the river. I lick my thumb and stamp the eye of a fighting rhinoceros. Its heavy head is already there in the stone, lowered and ready to gore the other rhinoceros.

And still another animal charges in the rock. There is a wrinkle in the rock. It looks just like the fold beneath the bison's shoulder where a hunter must throw the spear to pierce the lung. Tomorrow I shall kill the bison!

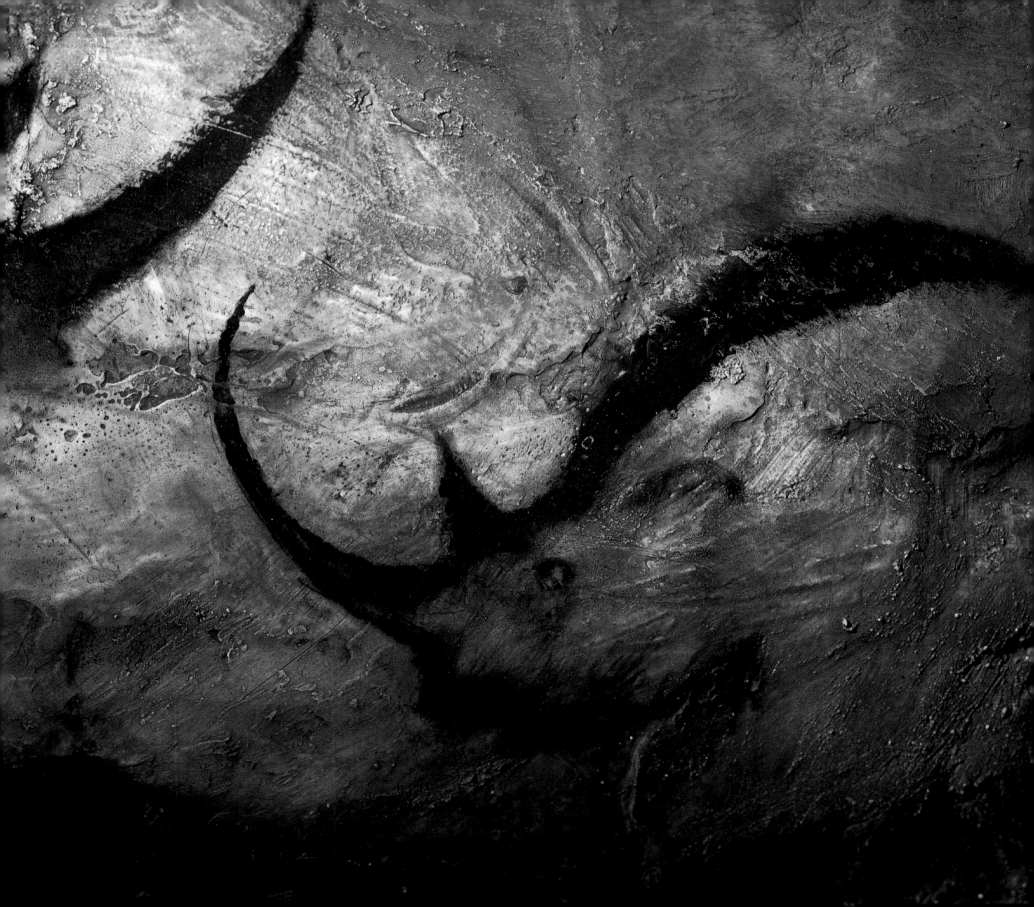

I begin with the wrinkle, and then I remember the rest of the bison easily. Above I paint a spear. It is the spear of my father. I use some dried moss to dab a shadow where the belly is. The shadow gives the belly roundness. It is a big bison, a fat bison. I let the rock show through the sponged marks, for the rock is the color of fat. My mouth waters! I suddenly remember how the blood sprays through the bison's muzzle when the hunters bring it down. Carefully I make a patch of red dots.

For three days I work. The last figure is one I've never seen, yet is one I know. The rock shows me the head, the claws, the powerful legs of the she-tiger. When I am about to leave I have a sudden thought and press my painting hand to the rock wall.

I turn to go and crawl out of the cave into the light of the rising sun. I look east and blink at familiar shapes rolling up in the sky. They look immense and woolly against the horizon. They are clouds, clouds that move like mammoths. Have I painted so long that in my mind's eye the two worlds now blur?

But even from a distance I can see my people, can see them standing with their heads tipped up toward the onrushing clouds. They must see what I see. The clouds must be real. My dream has finally caught!

When I get back to my clan's campsite the rain has started.

"Erloo!" I spot my sister, her thin body bent by the wet breeze like a blade of winter grass.

"Dream Catcher!" she shouts, and looks at my hands stained with the colors that I have painted on the cave wall. She runs to embrace me. The paint smears onto her bony shoulders as I hold her.

The others stare at the rain that falls in huge fat droplets. They close their eyes and tip their heads toward the sky and let the water run down their faces. I see a baby, stunned by the wetness, crouching to watch the raindrops, while another watches the rain make tiny rivers on his arm, and another blinks to catch the drops on his eyelashes.

Now the grass has come back, and the animals follow the grass, and the people follow the animals, and we are hungry no more. My sister's arms have grown fat and are no longer like twigs.

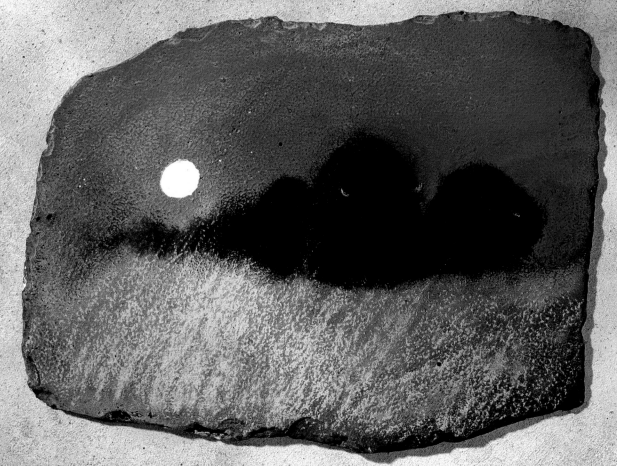

But still I go to the cave of the she-tiger to paint where the walls move with shadows and where, buried in the rock, are the shapes of animals, the sinew of the bison and the speed of the horses. I want to feel their strength, to touch their muscle. I want to draw everything. I want to paint!

AFTERWORD

First Painter is an imaginative reconstruction of a most elusive historical moment — the birth of the artistic imagination.

Cave paintings have been found throughout the world. In Europe, especially, the art in the caves of Lascaux, Altamira, Les Trois Frères, and Chauvet has become synonymous with the Cro-Magnon, those early modern human beings who lived between 35,000 and 12,000 years ago. It was at this time that modern human beings began to flourish and new forms of artistic expression appeared in their tools, their bodily ornamentation, and their clothing.

The cave of the she-tiger to which Mishoo goes is a composite of many caves found in France and Spain. It is most heavily based on the Chauvet cave in the Ardèche region of France. Discovered in December of 1994 by Jean-Marie Chauvet, Eliette Brunel-Deschamps, and Christian Hillaire, it contains paintings considered to be the most significant find in paleolithic art. Painted about 30,000 years ago, they are the oldest known cave paintings, distinctive for many reasons. Never in this region of France had cave art been found that depicted animals such as rhinoceroses, big cats, and bears. The paintings at Chauvet also display sophisticated techniques of perspective and movement, such as the horses with many legs—evidence that overturns the idea that cave art is merely the primitive expression of a primitive people.

Little is known about these paintings—who painted them or what inspired them. Were they just for decoration? Were they part of a ritual? Or a way of invoking spirits? Because of the inaccessibility of many of the caves, experts feel that they were probably meant to be viewed by only a few people, sometimes under difficult conditions where animals could be a threat.

No one knows the identity or even the gender of any of these cave painters. I have chosen to make the First Painter an adolescent girl who goes to the cave for spiritual reasons. Thus, I created Mishoo for this story.

To our ancient ancestors and the animal spirits—K.L. and R.B. And to my wife, Colleen, with love—R.B.

ACKNOWLEDGMENT

All the artwork was photographed by José Crespo.

BIBLIOGRAPHY

Bahn, Paul G.; Vertut, Jean. IMAGES OF THE ICE AGE. New York: Facts on File, 1988.

Campbell, Joseph. THE WAY OF THE ANIMAL POWERS. New York: Harper & Row, 1988.

Chauvet, Jean-Marie; Brunel-Deschamps, Eliette; Hillaire, Christian. DAWN OF ART: THE CHAUVET CAVE: THE OLDEST KNOWN PAINTINGS IN THE WORLD. New York: Harry N. Abrams, 1996.

Clottes, Jean; Williams, David Lewis. THE SHAMANS OF PREHISTORY: TRANCE AND MAGIC IN THE PAINTED CAVES. New York: Harry N. Abrams, 1988.

Gowlett, John. ASCENT TO CIVILIZATION: THE ARCHAEOLOGY OF EARLY MAN. New York: Alfred Knopf, 1984.

Janson, H.W. JANSON'S STORY OF PAINTING: FROM CAVE PAINTINGS TO MODERN TIMES. New York: Harry N. Abrams, 1984.

Lauber, Patricia. PAINTERS OF THE CAVES. Washington, D.C.: The National Geographic Society, 1998.

Lewin, Roger. HUMAN EVOLUTION, AN ILLUSTRATED INTRODUCTION. New York: W.H. Freeman & Co., 1984.

Lewin, Roger. THREAD OF LIFE: THE SMITHSONIAN LOOKS AT EVOLUTION. Washington, D.C.:Smithsonian Books, 1982.

Sattler, Helen Roney. HOMINIDS, A LOOK BACK AT OUR ANCESTORS. New York: Lothrop, Lee and Shepard, 1988.

Vialou, Denis. PREHISTORIC ART AND CIVILIZATION. New York: Harry N. Abrams, 1998.

A Melanie Kroupa Book

Ink

Dorling Kindersley Publishing, Inc.
95 Madison Avenue
New York, New York 10016

Visit us on the World Wide Web at
http://www.dk.com

Dorling Kindersley books are available at special
discounts for bulk purchases for sales promotions or
premiums. Special editions, including personalized
covers, excerpts of existing guides, and corporate
imprints, can be created in large quantities for specific
needs. For more information, contact Special Markets
Dept., Dorling Kindersley Publishing, Inc., 95 Madison
Avenue, New York, NY 10016; fax: (800) 600-9098.

Library of Congress Cataloging-in-Publication Data
Lasky, Kathryn.
First painter / by Kathryn Lasky; illustrated by Rocco
Baviera.—1st ed.
p. cm.
Summary: Following the death of her mother, Mishoo,
the new shaman, must find a way to help her prehis-
toric tribe during a drought.
ISBN 0-7894-2578-5
[1. Cave paintings—Fiction. 2. Prehistoric peoples—
Fiction.]
I. Baviera, Rocco, ill. II. Title.
PZ7.L3274Fi   2000   [Fic]—dc21
98-41154 – CIP   AC

Book design by Chris Hammill Paul.
The illustrations for this book were created using
watercolors, raw earth pigments, charcoal, bear
grease, animal fur, and plaster.
The text of this book is set in 14 point Maiandra
and Gill Sans.
Printed and bound in U.S.A.
First Edition, 2000
10 9 8 7 6 5 4 3 2 1